I raced through the school from the music rooms to the gym. No one was in the halls. No one was in the locker room either. I dropped by books on the bench by my locker and reached for my lock. My hand found only air; the lock was gone.

I glanced up and down the alcove of lockers. There was no sign of my lock anywhere. In my mind I heard a time clock ticking loudly and saw Mr. Zindorf looking very unhappy, yelling, "Where's McCarver?" I finally found my lock hanging backward on a lock at the far end of the room. I didn't need many brains to figure out what was going on: Rand . . .

7th Grade Soccer Star

GAYLE ROPER

Chariot Books
David C. Cook Publishing Co.

A White Horse Book
Published by Chariot Books,
an imprint of David C. Cook Publishing Co.
David C. Cook Publishing Co., Elgin, Illinois 60120
David C. Cook Publishing Co., Weston, Ontario

SEVENTH GRADE SOCCER STAR

Cover illustration by Paul Turnbaugh
Cover design by Loran Berg
First Print, 1988
Printed in the United States of America
92 91 90 89 5 4 3 2

Library of Congress Cataloging-in-Publication Data

Roper, Gayle G.
Seventh grade soccer star

(A Sports story for boys) (A White horse book)
Summary: An adopted boy seeks God's help in dealing with his feelings of being rejected by his birth mother and facing up to a bully on his junior high soccer team.
[1. Adoption—Fiction. 2. Soccer—Fiction. 3. Christian life—Fiction] I. Title. II. Title: 7th grade soccer star. III. Series.
PZ7.R6788Se 1988 [Fic] 88-9496
ISBN 1-55513-507-2

For Mom Gordinier,
Chip and Jeff,
and young Nate
—the special adopted people in my life.

1

I flopped back in my seat on the school bus and muttered under my breath. I, Jason McCarver, was the first one on and the last one off. It wasn't fair somehow. I slid over to make room for Mike.

"Did you hear what Mrs. Stevens said to me in English?" asked Mike. "She told me I wrote like her three-year-old—unreadable gibberish. Doesn't she realize how lucky she is to have a genius like me in her class?"

I leaned over and pulled a piece of paper from Mike's notebook. "Looks to me like she's right," I said. I pointed to the ink markings that traced their way across Mike's paper; they didn't look like any letters I'd ever seen.

"Does this actually say something?"

"That's a list of my homework for tomorrow."

I turned the paper around carefully. "Since we're in the same classes, it's also a list of my homework, right?"

I pointed to a word. "What's that?"

"History. See? There's the H."

I squinted carefully, then shook my head. "Mrs. Stevens is right; it looks like gibberish."

I handed the paper back. "We're in the big time now, Mike. Junior high. I don't think they're going to cater to your genius the way they did last year."

"Their loss," said Mike as he stuffed the paper back in his notebook.

"Get your dad to buy you that word processing program you were reading about last week. I think you're going to need it to pass English."

"It won't improve the caliber of my work one iota."

"Maybe not, but at least Mrs. Stevens will be able to read it."

Mike pulled out his history paper again. "It's not that bad," he defended himself. "All she has to do is be creative. It'll be a good exercise in stretching her mind and her imagination. She'll be thanking me before June gets here."

But I wasn't listening to Mike anymore. I was watching Mary Ellen Lafferty three seats ahead. She was amazing. All the other girls in seventh grade were either lumpy and dumpy, or so tall and lanky that I bumped into their knees every time I turned around. But Mary Ellen was—Mary Ellen.

Her red-gold hair was combed back and fastened with a barrette, falling in a golden waterfall down her back. The little wisps that had worked their way free after a day in school curled softly at her forehead. All the other girls' hair looked as if they'd combed it with egg beaters.

"She'll never be around by the time I'm allowed to date," I said pessimistically. "Never. Not with eyes like that."

Mike looked at Mary Ellen's gorgeous violet eyes without interest. "How long will that be?"

"Three years." No matter how much I pleaded, my parents held to their rule—no single dates until I was sixteen.

"That rule's for old-fashioned girls," said Mike.

"Tell me about it."

Sometimes I wished my parents didn't care about me so much. They tended to get in my way. Not that they were bad or unkind, but on a scale from one to ten, ten being highest, they were somewhere around a six. Except on certain days when they were definitely zeros.

Of course I was thankful I didn't have Mike's parents. They were zeros all the time, fighting like they did. If words were bats, they'd have beaten each other to death long ago.

As a result, Mike's parents didn't have much time for him and he had a lot of freedom. All summer he'd been able to run around long after dark when I had to be in, and he never had to go to church.

Mike pulled out his crumpled computer magazine and pointed in Mary Ellen's direction. "Even I know she won't be around for you in three years, and I don't know anything about girls."

I sighed deeply. I tore my eyes away from Mary Ellen before she realized I was staring and looked at Mike's ratty magazine.

"How can you read that computer stuff all the time?"

"I love bits and bytes, and learning how to be the world's greatest hacker."

I shook my head. "No good, Mike. You need to get outside more." I blinked; I sounded just like my father. "Come over today and we'll work on the clubhouse."

Mike shrugged. "Okay. It's better than staying home."

"If you don't want to stay home, why don't you go out for soccer with me? We'd have a great time!" The frown on his face did not discourage me. "This is a terrific idea," I said enthusiastically. "You could be the team manager."

"Manager!" he said in surprise. "I hate sports. All you do is run around and get hurt."

He paused and I could tell he was thinking about the prospect.

"What's a manager do?" he asked.

"Managers manage," I said. "Think about it.

We'd have a great time being on the team together."

Mike went back to reading his magazine. I settled back to watch Mary Ellen discreetly until she got off the bus.

A crumpled paper ball startled me as it whizzed past my ear and landed in my lap. A second one hit me in the back of the head even before the first one stopped bouncing. I grabbed at the first one and spun around ready to fire.

Smiling wildly at me was Judy Post.

"Oh, it's only you." I dropped my arm and let the paper fall to the floor. Why did this girl have to like me? She had been actively pursuing me for the past three years. I'd been flattered the first week back in fourth grade, but the "honor" had long since worn off. No matter what I did, she refused to take the hint and leave me alone.

"What a nice greeting," said Judy with a phony pout.

My stomach curdled.

She patted the empty seat beside her. "Why don't you come sit beside me?"

Over my dead body.

"I can't. I'm sitting with Mike."

"He'll never miss you."

I looked at him. How true. "I just can't leave him. I promised I'd ride with him all year," I lied. "He's afraid some girl might sit next to him."

"So who'd ever sit next to him?" said Judy in disgust.

I was stung. Mike might be a bit wierd, but no one was allowed to talk about him like that but me.

"Watch your mouth, Judy. You're no treasure yourself."

Now it was Judy's turn to be upset. No matter what she said to me, I was mean to her and she didn't like it.

"What do you mean 'I'm no great treasure'?" Her voice was loud because she was upset.

Goaded by three years of aggravation, I spoke frankly. "You're a pain in the neck, Judy. You're pushy, you're loud, and . . ."

I glanced quickly at Mary Ellen and saw her lovely face laughing at something her friend had said, then swung back to look at Judy with her zits and crooked teeth and frowzy hair.

". . . And you're ugly!"

I regretted what I'd said as soon as the words were out of my mouth. Even I knew I had gone too far. In my mind I could see my mother's horrified face. I felt really bad as I watched Judy's face turn a painful red.

"I'm sorry," I began, but embarrassed anger flowed from Judy in a flood that washed away my weak apology.

"I may be no great treasure and I may be ugly," she said vehemently, pointing her finger in my face, "but at least I'm not a reject like you! At least I'm not adopted!"

2

I was numb from shock and outrage as I walked home from the bus stop. I could still feel the hot flush of mortification that swept over me as I slouched in my seat trying to hide from all the curious eyes. The only one not staring was Mike, lost in that stupid computer magazine of his. Even Mary Ellen had turned to stare.

Surely death by torture would be easier than what I'd suffered.

How had Judy known I was adopted?

Why did she have to yell it to the whole world?

How could I ever face people tomorrow?

Mary Ellen would definitely write me off as a loser now—Jase-the-Reject. When I finally did turn sixteen, no one would go out with me, especially Mary Ellen. Only Judy.

I pulled the front door open and tried to slip past Mom to my room. No success.

"Hi, Jase," she called from the kitchen. She has better ears than a rabbit. "How was your day?"

I scrunched my face up in a silent scream. The last thing I wanted to talk about was my day.

"Great," I called and fled to my room. I threw my books on the desk and flopped on the bed.

"*At least I'm not a reject like you! At least I'm not adopted!*"

It wasn't that Judy's taunt had told me something I hadn't known. I'd known I was adopted since I was a little kid. One of Mom's favorite stories, the cutesy kind you swear you were never stupid enough to do, was about the time when I was five and thought a person was either born or adopted, not both.

And there were the slides that documented the story of how Mom and Dad had gone to the adoption agency to get me and all their joy and stuff. My little brother Matty had a series like that, too.

In fact, I could still remember when we went to court to finalize Matty's adoption. He was sitting on Mom's lap, rocking back and forth like little kids do, when all of a sudden he lost his balance and hit his face against the table where we were sitting.

He bled all over the judge's chambers. I remember lots of red. And some wild lady who worked there put me in a chair, telling me that if I moved, I'd get it.

But even though I knew I was adopted, I didn't talk about it outside the house. It made me feel too different, too odd, too uncomfortable.

There was a knock at my door.

"Jase, may I come in?" asked Mom.

I wished I had the courage to say no because I wanted to be alone, but I said, "Yes."

Mom walked in all smiles and sunshine. "Tell me about your day. Do you like junior high? How are your teachers? Guess what? Matty has Mr. Jeffries just as you did in fifth grade."

She looked at me expectantly; I looked back. It was like looking at a stranger. Sometimes I felt so disconnected from this family.

"So tell me," she prompted.

I shrugged. "It was okay. Mike's in all of my classes. Band looks like it's going to be good. Mr. Keefer, the director, seems like a nice man. And I think I'll be able to make first chair trumpet."

"But, Jase, you're only in seventh grade."

"Yeah, but the ninth grade guys are terrible, and the only eighth grader is a girl who spends all her time worrying about her lipstick. You can't play the trumpet and think about lipstick." I nodded confidently. "Don't worry; I'll make it."

"I'm not worried, but don't overestimate your ability. I don't want you to get hurt."

Oh, Mom, I thought, you don't realize how

important music is to me and how good I am.

"How about soccer?" she asked. She loved sports.

"Soccer tryouts for the seventh and eighth grade teams are next Tuesday."

"You won't have any trouble there," Mom said confidently. "You play so well."

"Sure, Mom. And none of the other guys do."

"Don't be flip, Jase. You know what I mean. What else happened today?"

She waited, but I said nothing. I wasn't about to tell her about Judy.

After a couple of minutes, Mom shrugged. "By the way, you never finished cleaning the basement yesterday. I want you to finish before you get involved in anything else."

"But Mike's coming over and we're going to work on our clubhouse."

"I'm certain he won't mind helping you or waiting for you to finish."

"But I've got lots of homework!"

"Your first day? You've got time to finish one chore."

"Did you ever realize how certain you are about the things that have to do with me, yet you never check with me?"

Mom looked at me with her right eyebrow cocked. "My, my, you're in fine fettle today. Just do as you're asked."

"Just do as you're asked," I muttered under my breath as she turned and went out of the room. I lay on my bed and stared at the ceiling.

A chirp from the cage in the corner roused me from my sulk. It came from Petey, the blue and white parakeet that Mom and Dad had bought me for my last birthday.

"Hey, Petey, did you miss me?"

I climbed off the bed and opened the bird cage. Petey hopped out onto my finger. Chirruping happily, the bird walked up my arm and sat on my shoulder. He reached out and tweaked my ear, his version of a kiss.

Together we went to the basement. I gave the floor a quick once-over, sweeping some of the dirt under the rug. I didn't feel like getting rid of it properly.

By the time Mike arrived, I was finished and we ran out to the woods behind our houses. Mike and I had been neighbors as long as I could remember, and our friendship had survived growing up together.

"You ought to put Petey back in his cage," Mike said as we inspected the work we had done on our clubhouse. "One day he's going to fly away."

"Not my boy," I said as I stroked Petey's breast. "Besides, his wings are clipped."

Petey sidled along my collar until he was at the back of my neck. Then he leaned forward, burying himself in my hair, and stayed there for the whole time Mike and I worked on our clubhouse.

When Mom called me for dinner, I was surprised

at how fast the afternoon had gone. I'd even forgotten Judy. I went to the table with a huge appetite.

Everyone shared what had happened during their day. Dad's boss, Mr. Tyler, was a man who told terrible jokes all the time, and he'd told a new one at the staff meeting that morning. We all laughed when Dad repeated it; it was so bad. Mom told about meeting some former neighbors at the store and caught us up on all their news. I gave a brief and selected version of my day. Mostly Matty talked about how marvelous Mr. Jeffries was.

"He has the best learning centers in the school, he organized us in teams and pitched to us at recess, and his jokes are definitely better than Mr. Tyler's, Dad. Jase, he told me how pleased he was to have another McCarver."

In spite of my glums, I was pleased. I'd liked Mr. Jeffries and he had liked me.

"Guess what?" Matty continued.

Matty was always talking, his blue eyes jumping from person to person, his reddish hair and freckles bouncing up and down as he nodded his head, agreeing with whatever he was saying. I liked the kid in spite of the fact that we were brothers.

"In a month we're going to have Heritage Day. Mr. Jeffries told us early so that we'd have lots of time to learn about where we came from and get costumes ready because we're going to have a parade! The whole school is going to have a Heritage Day parade!"

"Sounds great, Matty," said Dad. "You can have fun going as a McCarver and wearing a Scottish kilt. I think our family came to America around 1900, but we'll have to look it up to be certain. Grandma McCarver has lots of family information."

"Phoo," said Mom. "They're late comers, those McCarvers. You want to go as a Gardinier, honey. We were here before the Revolutionary War. In fact, we even fought in it. Great-great-great-however-many-greats Grandfather Gardinier was a captain in the revolutionary army. You can be a Gardinier and go dressed as an old time soldier."

"But be careful," said Dad. "There's a vicious rumor going around that the Gardiniers were chicken thieves in the old days. You'd be throwing yourself in with a questionable group."

Matty laughed and I was interested in spite of myself.

"Was your family really a bunch of thieves?" Matty asked Mom.

"Many generations ago. It's written up in *American Heritage* in an article about Old New York, Grandpa Gardinier tells me. He's got a copy of the article." Mom smiled. "You didn't know you had such famous ancestors, did you?"

"Infamous is more like it," Dad said.

"I still don't know if I've got famous ancestors," said Matty matter-of-factly. "That's your ancestors, not mine, and I really don't know whose roots I should go as—Dad's, yours, or mine."

3

I had to admit that Mom and Dad barely flinched at Matty's unexpected comment.

"That's an interesting thought, Matty, going as your own heritage," said Mom. "I wish we knew more about your parents, but we don't have much information."

"Why don't you?" asked Matty as he used his thumb to get all his peas collected on his plate. The kid had terrible table manners.

"Adoption agencies usually keep information about the adoptive families and the birth families very general so they can't trace each other. It's supposed to be for everyone's protection."

"I can see why they might not want the mother to

know where her baby went so that she can't come and get him or something," said Matty, "but why can't we know about her?"

I looked at Matty. Sometimes he could be so stupid.

"So you can't pop in on her unannounced," I said. "She might not want people to know about you."

"Why not?" asked Matty. "I'm a nice kid. Just ask Mom."

"Because she probably wasn't married when she had you, that's why. You'd be an embarrassment to her. I'd be an embarrassment to my mother, too."

The anger and hurt from Judy's nasty reject crack showed in my voice. Mom and Dad looked concerned, but I didn't care.

"Oh," said Matty, unimpressed. "I see what you mean. Do you remember Palmer Hardin in my class, the brainiak who always complains about everything? His older sister is going to have a baby and she's not married. He says his father isn't speaking to her, and the baby will be born in two months. Palmer says she's planning to keep the baby. His mom wants her to and his father doesn't."

Mom shook her head. "Poor girl. What a terrible situation. No matter what she does, she's got problems."

"Well," I said, my voice hard, "I don't feel sorry for her at all."

"I do," Mom continued. "She's too young for all the responsibilities of having a baby. I feel sorry for your moms, too, not knowing what you guys are like, what you're doing." Mom feels sorry for stray cats and sad looking dogs, too. "But I think your moms did the better thing in giving you up. Not only did they make Dad and me very happy, but they put you two in a stable home with a father who loves you."

Matty stabbed his last pea. "Sometimes I wonder what my father and mother are like," he said. "How old are they? Would they let me get away with more than you guys do? Are they rich? Would they buy me an all-terrain cycle?"

"Do you ever feel you'd like to meet your parents some day?" Dad asked.

Matty wiped his milk mustache off with the napkin Mom shoved in his hand. "Sometimes," he said, "especially when I'm mad at you."

"How about you, Jase?" Dad asked.

"Why should I want to meet them?" I snapped, my heart beating so angrily I thought it'd pop out of my chest. "It's their fault I'm a reject!"

Mom and Dad stared at me. Even Matty stopped eating for a moment.

"A reject?" Mom said. "Whatever gave you that idea!"

I stood up and threw my napkin down. It landed very unsatisfactorily. I wished I could throw a glass or something. The explosion when it hit would be worthy of my feelings.

"You know my mother didn't want me!" I

shouted. "Don't play games! She just gave me up and some lady at the adoption agency called and said, "Come get this kid,' and you had to pick me up. There you were, stuck with the reject!"

I made a dash for my room, but Dad grabbed me as I passed him.

"Sit down, Jase."

I slumped in my chair, suddenly tired.

"First, let me rid you of the reject idea," he said. "Neither you nor Matty is a reject. If ever kids were wanted, you two were."

Mom nodded her head enthusiastically. "We prayed for you two for a very long time. We went out of our way to get you. Any adopted child is a wanted baby, more so than many natural children. Don't ever forget that!"

I didn't say anything. I wasn't certain that what they said made me feel better, but it didn't make me feel any worse.

"And we know your mother cared for you, Jase." Mom's voice got soft and she reached out and patted my hand. "She knit you a sweater and booties while carrying you and then sent them with you when you left the hospital."

I nodded. I had heard the story before, seen the sweater, though not the booties—at least not that I remember. I'm told I flushed them down the toilet one day when I was two. But it did help to know that she'd spent that time on me.

"Did my mother send anything?" asked Matty.

"No," said Mom. "Does that bother you?"

Matty thought a minute. "Nope. It really doesn't. I don't think being adopted is any big deal."

I stared at the kid. No big deal! Was he crazy? Didn't he feel full of nagging, unanswered questions?

Matty kept talking. "I've always figured God knew what He was doing. You guys were praying for a baby. God gave me to you. If He arranged it, it's okay with me."

Mom and Dad smiled.

"But," said Matty and their smiles dimmed a little, "I still wish I knew about my background so I'd know what to be on Heritage Day. What if I could wear a really neat costume?"

"A kilt is a great costume," said Dad. "Going as a McCarver would let you wear one."

"Dad, I don't mind being a McCarver, but a kilt's a skirt!"

"I've got an idea, Matty," said Mom. "Why don't we write to the adoption agency and ask them for all the information they can give us about your parents? We'll ask for yours, too, Jase. Then maybe both of you can get some questions answered."

Matty was excited about the idea. "Will they tell us much stuff?"

"We'll have to see," Mom said. "Most of it will probably be non-identifying things. I know they told us things when we got you both, but we were so excited that we've forgotten most of it. I do remember that Jase's father was an athlete and his mother a musician. And Matty's mother was a high school junior. But that's not much to build your sense of background on. Let's clean up the dinner mess and then I'll write the letter."

More information about my birth parents. The idea made my stomach feel funny. On one hand I wanted to know more about them so I'd know more about me. On the other hand, I was scared about what I'd learn.

4

I raced around the soccer field with zillions of other guys. In my wildest dreams I'd never expected this many people to try out for the team. I guess I was too used to community leagues where they just added another team if there were too many players. The old give-everybody-a-chance-to-play routine was not going to work here.

Since three grade schools sent kids to this junior high, I wasn't certain how many of the guys panting with me were trying out for the seventh grade team. I'd never seen most of them before. Say half for seventh, half for eighth (the freshmen went to the high school for the J-V team). My heart sank. That was an awful lot of competition.

After we'd run ten laps of the field, the coaches separated us into graded teams, and I discovered that two-thirds of the kids were in seventh grade. I guess by eighth grade they've weeded out the ones who aren't serious.

My stomach kept running laps around my insides as I tried to look casual and confident. The giant standing beside me did nothing to help me out.

"Hey, little man," he said, hardly panting at all. "Are you sure you're strong enough to kick that big soccer ball?"

My eyes were even with his armpits, and I didn't think it would be a good idea to tell him that I'd made the All-County team and that we'd finished third in the state in the community league last season. It'd probably turn out he was an All-American or something.

Mr. Zindorf, the coach, began dividing us up according to the position we wanted to play. There were thirty—thirty!—who wanted to be forward, including me and the giant. Twelve guys were interested in halfback, eight in fullback, and no one in goalie.

Soon we were running up and down the field as everyone got a chance to prove his abilities for the position he wanted. I tried to flash my quick feet for Mr. Z., but it was difficult for him to be impressed by my goal when there was no goalie.

We finished up with some drills and more jogging. By the griping around me, I knew we were going to loose some of my competition by tomorrow, if they didn't keel over today.

"How'd it go, Jase?" Dad asked at dinner.

"I think okay, but there are some good kids out there. And some big ones, too."

"Then there's no problem," said Mom. "You're very good, and size isn't the issue in soccer. Speed is."

There she was, being confident for me again. "Yeah, but don't forget that these big guys have longer legs and can really run."

Mom shrugged. "You'll be growing, too, you know."

"Sure, someday maybe. These guys have already grown. This one guy looks like seven feet."

Matty was staring at me through slitted eyes, making me fidget.

"What?" I demanded. "What?"

"Are you going to be tall?" he asked.

"How do I know? Who cares?" But I did care and I had wondered a lot. Sometimes I felt I could do with a little less brain and a little more brawn.

"I never thought about it before," said Matty, "but Jase and I don't know how tall we'll be. If Dad was our father and Granddad and Grandpa our grandfathers, we'd at least have some idea, but we don't have any guide at all. What if Jase never grows? What if he's one of those skinny little guys that they kick sand on?" Matty laughed.

If my arms were longer, I'd have reached across

the table and bopped him one. Instead, I changed the subject and told them about the great goal I'd made for Mr. Zindorf, neglecting to tell them there was no goalie at the time.

By Friday, twenty-three kids had dropped out. We had a scrimmage game against the eighth grade team and got clobbered, but I scored a point. So did the giant whose name was Rand Purcell.

"Hey, little man," Rand sneered after I scored my goal. "What a lucky break."

Later when I ran after the ball, instead of trying to set up to receive my pass, Rand raced out of position and took the ball from me, making certain to throw his hip at me so that I fell.

I somersaulted and jumped back up right away, but Rand and the ball were long gone. I glanced at Mr. Zindorf, not knowing what he had seen, not sure whether I should say anything.

The next time Rand walked by me, he looked at me and laughed in a very nasty way.

I had decided the first day that I didn't like Rand, and nothing was happening to change my mind. He was a bully, and for some reason he'd chosen me for a target. Mike told me it was because I was good and therefore a threat. Some threat. It was like a humming bird having a competition with an eagle. Three guesses who the humming bird was.

"He's such a jerk!" I told Mike Saturday as we worked on the clubhouse.

"Don't worry," Mike assured me. "Mr. Zindorf

saw him take you out the other day."

"Are you sure? He didn't say anything."

"Hey, I'm a manager, right? My job is to follow the coach around and do whatever he tells me. I know he saw everything. I was right beside him."

I felt a little better, but the idea of playing on the forward line with Rand on a regular basis made me feel ill. I'd always had great fun with soccer before. Now because some big monster liked to throw his weight around, my fun level was zero. I even thought about quitting.

"You can't quit!" Mike was furious at the suggestion. "I'm a manager for this stupid team because you're on it. I'd rather read my magazines or play with my computer, but you got me to volunteer in a weak moment. You can't drop out now and leave me alone!"

I grinned. "You could quit, too."

Mike stood tall, almost as tall as me—which isn't saying much. "Quitting has no class," he stated, then wilted quickly to naturalness. "That's what my mother says to my father every time he tells her that if she doesn't like things, she should just do him a favor and leave. 'You can't get rid of me that easily, John,' she screams. 'Besides, quitting has no class!' " Mike made a face. "I always feel like saying, 'And yelling does?' "

Poor Mike. No wonder he hung around our house all the time. In fact, he was hanging around at dinner and was puppy dog happy when Mom asked him to eat with us. He was even glad when she invited him to go to church with us the next night.

"It'll be the official start of being in the junior high youth group, Mike. I know you'll love it as much as Jase will."

At least it was better than regular church. We were allowed to play around for awhile and we sang some up-to-date songs instead of the dead hymns we sing Sunday mornings. The guy in charge, Pastor Tony, the youth pastor, only spoke half as long as Pastor Harrison in the mornings.

Best of all they announced a canoe trip down Sedgewick's Run in two weeks. I could just imagine Mary Ellen in the front of my canoe, smiling sweetly, her long hair trailing gently in the water as I paddled into the sunset. Unfortunately I was certain I'd never have the nerve to ask her, but it was a rich dream I could use to block out towering, terrifying giants named Rand.

"Can I come to this meeting thing again?" asked Mike on the way home. "That was great!"

"Sure," said Dad. "No trouble at all. What did you like best?"

"All of it," said Mike. He nodded earnestly. "It was great."

I stared at my friend. Enough was enough already. But Mike kept on leaning over the front seat talking to Mom and Dad.

"I even learned something new—besides the songs, I mean. Pastor Tony said that God is with me everywhere. Is that right? I mean, I sort of knew that God was everywhere or He wouldn't be God, but I never thought about Him being with *me*. Because if He's with *me* everywhere, then He's with me at home and I'm not alone in that mess after all."

I looked at Mike as he and Mom and Dad kept talking. Every time he let something slip about how horrible things were in his home, I was taken by surprise. I knew it was bad there, but because I hardly ever went in, I kept forgetting. It would be nice for him to know that God was with him everywhere.

"What ramifications!" said genius Mike. He might not be able to spell and he couldn't write, but he loved long words. His favorite was extrapolation, and he refused to tell me what it meant. Some day I might look it up in a dictionary.

"What ramifications," he repeated. "God goes to work with you, Mr. McCarver; He goes wherever you go, Mrs. McCarver; He's in fifth grade with Matty, and He's on the soccer field with Jase. He even goes home with me. If He's there—everywhere, I mean—He takes care of us, right?"

"Even in the bad times," said Dad.

Mike never wound down the whole way home. He was still chattering when we dropped him off at his house. I fell asleep hearing Mike's voice in my imagination and woke seeing Rand's face in a nightmare. I was the soccer ball and Rand was kicking me down the field.

When school ended Monday, Mike and I walked across the locker room and out to the soccer field. Rand trailed us menacingly.

"Today's the day I really show you how to play," he hissed at me.

Mike leaned close. "Don't worry, Jase. God is with you on the soccer field. He's everywhere."

I rolled my eyes and began jogging. Soon Rand was right at my feet, and the next thing I knew, he stepped on my heel. My shoe came off, I lost my rhythm and fell in a heap, skinning my knee.

"Eat my dust, kid," he called as he jogged past.

Mr. Zindorf called us all together. I had almost stopped bleeding as he looked us over.

"As you all know, we are having goalie troubles," he said. "None of you seems to want what may well be the most important job on the team. I guess it's not flashy enough."

He grinned as he spoke to let us know he wasn't put out or anything. He was a nice man. Maybe if I asked him, he'd beat up Rand for me.

"So I've come to the conclusion that I will just have to appoint one of you goalie."

We all looked at each other, hoping not to be his choice. Goalie could be so boring! And when you did get your chance, if you flubbed, everyone on the team hated you.

"My choice for goalie is a quick, agile player of great ability. I plan to make him the best goalie in the league. Rand Purcell, are you up to the challenge?"

Rand's face was a mess. He was upset and mad and afraid to show it. He'd obviously been picturing himself as high scorer and all-around hero.

"No, Mr. Zindorf. I'm a forward! I'm a good forward!"

"You are now a goalie, Rand. Congratulations."

I looked at Mike and smiled broadly. Goalies were tied to their cages. I was free of Rand. Suddenly soccer looked like fun again.

5

Tuesday was a bad day all the way around. First, I missed the school bus because I couldn't find my gym shorts. Second, I received a lecture from Mom as she drove me to school about responsibility and preparing the night before. I also got a lecture from the vice principal on how anyone in junior high should be beyond lateness. Then I realized I'd left my trumpet at home and I sure couldn't go to the first band practice with nothing to play. Next, as I was getting my stuff out of my locker, I realized I'd forgotten my lunch. Quickly searching my pockets, I found thirty cents. I couldn't even buy milk and a bag of chips!

To make matters worse, Mrs. Stevens gave us

these horrible vocabulary books and promised us a test weekly and aren't we glad we're able to supplement our education in so fine a manner? After all, college is just around the corner.

But it was at lunch that a truly terrible thing happened.

Mike and I had begun eating with a couple of the guys in our class who were also on the soccer team, Jeremy and Fonz (his real name is Alphonso, but he'll kill if he hears anyone call him that). If I sat just right at our regular table, I could see Mary Ellen who always ate at the same place with her friends.

Jeremy and Fonz were almost as delighted as I was that Mr. Zindorf had made Rand goalie. While he had never mocked them to the degree he had me, they didn't like him either.

"He's such a bully," said Jeremy.

"If I had the nerve, I'd trip him just like he tripped you, Jase," said Fonz.

I grinned. Fonz was about as big as I was and the vision of him tripping and actually felling Rand was funny. I could see him getting his shin broken when Rand ran into it, rather than Rand going down.

"Why is he so obnoxious?" asked Mike. "There has to be a reason. You guys were in the same school with him last year. What do you know about him?"

The guys looked at each other and shrugged.

"He's always been big," said Fonz.

"And he's always been a bully," said Jeremy.

"I pity any little brothers or sisters," I said.

"There aren't any," said Fonz. "He's an only kid, and he hasn't got a father."

"Aha!" said Mike. "His father ran out and he's mad at the world."

"I don't know about his father running out," said Fonz. "I don't think he ever had one. His mom was never married.

"I remember that Rand was always getting into trouble in school because he's such a bully, and his mom would never show up when they called her to come in. My mom works in the school office, and I heard her talking about it more than once. She said that Rand's mom was only sixteen when he was born."

"Only sixteen?" I thought a minute. "She was probably in tenth grade, only three years older than we are."

"Why'd she ever have him in the first place?" Jeremy said. "She could have had an abortion and saved us all a lot of trouble."

"Hey," I said. "Don't talk about abortions. My birth mom could have had one, too, and then where would I be?"

"Your birth mom?" said Jeremy. "Are you adopted or something?"

I nodded.

Jeremy shook his head. "No, you're not."

"Yes, I am."

Mike nodded eagerly. "Yes, he is."

"Wasn't your mom married either?" asked Fonz.

"I don't know," I said, already regretting that I'd ever mentioned me. "I don't know anything about her."

"Aren't you curious?" asked Jeremy.

My heart was starting to race again like it did whenever I talked about my adoption. Granted, I was glad my birth mother hadn't had an abortion, but that didn't mean I wanted to talk about her. I changed the subject to our vocabulary books and we spent a happy ten minutes complaining about Mrs. Stevens.

It seemed to me that at lunch I had the best of both worlds—the guys to fool around with and Mary Ellen to worship from afar. I watched her over Jeremy's shoulder as we laughed and dissected Mrs. Paton. This day Mary Ellen had on a vest with a wooly sheep grazing on its front. The sheep had a red bow tied around his neck, and she had a bow in her hair that matched the sheep's. She looked beautiful.

Lunch was almost over when Rand Purcell approached Mary Ellen's table and began to talk with the girls. I couldn't hear a thing he was saying, but I could tell he was making a big impression by the way the girls kept giggling.

I tried to picture how Mary Ellen saw Rand, and I wasn't comforted. He was tall, handsome, and well developed. No one would ever kick sand on him at the beach.

Suddenly the girls all slid down and Rand sat in the empty space, right next to Mary Ellen. I watched as she blushed and smiled shyly. Talk about gorgeous! I sighed. The only positive thing I could say about Rand was that at least he had good taste in girls.

"Don't worry about him," Mike said suddenly. "He hasn't got a chance."

"Who?" said Jeremy. He turned around to see where we were looking. So did Fonz.

"Ah," said Fonz. "I wondered how long it would take Purcell to make a move on Mary Ellen. He's been a ladies' man since first grade. And if he hasn't got a chance, it'll be the first time. The girls fall all over themselves if he even looks their way."

"Must be tough," said Jeremy.

I watched sadly as the bell rang and Rand walked Mary Ellen to her next class. I had the opportunity to watch very closely because she was in my after lunch science class. I had to walk down the hall behind the two of them. She giggled and gave him a little wave as she turned into the room.

As I followed her, someone barged into me, trying to squeeze past in the doorway that wouldn't hold two. It was Judy. I hadn't spoken to her since the day on the bus. Now I was too sad about Mary Ellen to remember to be angry with Judy.

"Hi, Judy. Take your time. Mr. Freneau won't start without you."

Judy managed a little smile as she dropped into

her desk. Now, I thought sadly, I understand how she must feel about me not liking her. I looked at Judy again and felt my heart stir, not with affection, oh no!, but with sympathy and pity.

There were only five minutes left of the class when Mr. Freneau dropped his bomb, the second truly great catastrophe of the day.

"We are going to be studying genetics for the next month," he said. "Genetics is the biology of heredity. Why do you look like you do? Who do you look like? Do you have your grandfather's nose? Your Aunt Ida's hair? Why do you think the way you do?"

Great, I thought. Just what a reject like me needs to study. Family trees could only be interesting if you knew what tree you were a branch of. It was all I could do not to look in Judy's direction to see if she realized what heredity meant—or didn't mean—to someone like me.

Mr. Freneau continued, "As part of this area of study, I want each of you to trace your physical and emotional characteristics, your talents and abilities, in a sort of family tree."

I stared at the man, appalled. My heart was racing again. Not only was I going to hate the course of study, but I was being doomed to fail it! There was no way I could do what he asked! What was I supposed to do? Make up a family tree?

"For instance," Mr. Freneau said, "Mary Ellen here has red-blonde hair. Someone in her family must have similar hair. Is it just one person? Or is red-gold hair a major family trait?

"Or Mike here is a genius. Where does he get his extra brain power? His mom? His dad? His Great-Aunt Harriet?"

As the class laughed, I slouched as far down in my seat as I could. I knew they weren't laughing at me, but I felt like they could be. Old Jase-the-Reject, he doesn't even know if he has a Great-Aunt Harriet to take after.

"I'm not certain what to do," I wailed at the dinner table. "I feel so embarrassed by the whole thing."

"You could always tell him you're adopted and ask to be excused," said Matty.

"I can't do that! You've got to understand; this is a big grade."

"Then fudge it," the kid said. "You've got brown hair and brown eyes, so does Dad. And while Mom's hair's lighter, her eyes are brown, too. You obviously got your brains from me."

Mom and Dad laughed with Matty, but I didn't. The situation was too grave.

Matty ran his fingers through his red curls and his blue eyes were wide open. "I wonder if I'll have to do the same thing when I'm in seventh grade. I certainly can't pass myself off genetically on this family."

"You know," said Dad, "you can do as Matty

suggests, Jase. There are enough physical similarities for it to work."

I stared at my plate. I felt alone, like a man with leprosy in Bible times with people walking around him, no one talking to him or touching him.

"When's the project due?" asked Mom.

"Not for a few weeks."

"Then maybe there's really no problem," she said. "Maybe the information we sent for will arrive from the adoption agency in time for both Matty's Heritage Day and your report."

Somehow her words didn't comfort.

6

Wednesday after practice Dad stopped on his way home from work for Mike and me. Mr. Zindorf followed us to the car. We climbed in the back seat and he walked to the front window beside Dad.

"Mr. McCarver, may I speak with you a minute?" He stepped back from the car, and it was obvious he wanted to talk with Dad away from us.

"What can I do for you?" Dad said as he opened the front door.

I rolled down my window as quietly as I could. If they were going to talk about me, I wanted to hear it. I could almost feel my ear growing into a huge satellite dish as I strained to hear. Mike was doing the same thing.

"Do you know Rand Purcell?" Mr. Zindorf asked Dad.

Mike and I looked at each other and made a face.

"I've heard Jase talk about him," Dad said, sort of smiling. He was too nice to repeat all the nasty things I'd said.

Mr. Zindorf smiled back at Dad and then glanced at us. We quickly tried to look unaware.

"I'm sure Jase has talked about him," the coach said. "The boy can be a handful." Mr. Zindorf's face got very serious. "He has many problems, not the least of which is his home situation."

Mike and I looked at each other. No father.

"Just recently Rand's mother moved out of her parents' home where she'd lived all her life and into an apartment of her own at Maplewood. She took Rand with her even though her parents wanted him to stay with them. I'm very concerned for him."

"How can we help?" asked Dad.

Not in any way, I felt like yelling. Rand doesn't need or want our help. I looked at Mike and could see he felt the same way.

"I was wondering if you would be willing to drive Rand home after practices. I know Maplewood is out of your way a bit, but the kid is walking home alone every night. It's not too bad now with the weather still warm and the evenings still long, but soon it'll be cold and dark before he gets home."

Walking home every night! Three miles at least!

"I've been taking the boy home if I have time,"

said Mr. Zindorf, "but I live in the opposite direction."

Dad shrugged. "I see no problem with dropping him off. Just tell him to be out here waiting for me with Jase and Mike."

"Can you start tonight?" asked the coach.

"We can start tonight," said Dad.

The ride home was awkward. Rand sat up front with Dad. Instead of talking about practice and telling all the stupid and great things that had happened like we usually did, Mike and I sat staring daggers at the back of Rand's head while Dad tried to talk with him. All the big jerk said was, "Yeah" or "Uh-uh." Obviously conversation, if he wasn't pushing you around or flirting with the girls, wasn't one of his talents.

"Dad," I said after we got rid of Rand, "how could you say yes?"

"Jase, how could I say no?"

"There's such a thing as being too nice, you know."

Dad laughed. "I doubt it."

"Well, at least he can't beat me up with you in the car. Just don't ever be late."

It seemed that all of a sudden practices turned into games. We played the seventh grade team from Lymne Junior High away and won 3-1. I scored two goals, Fonz got one, and Rand was a hero in the net, racking up a bunch of saves. I didn't like to admit it, but he was a good goalie.

"I told you, Rand," said Mr. Zindorf, "you're going to be a great goalie."

In spite of himself, Rand was starting to like the position, especially since it was so obvious that he was good.

Our game the following week was at home against Concord Junior High. Mom and Matty came and Dad got there in time for the last fifteen minutes.

"Jase, you were terrific," said Matty after the game. "I kept telling the girl with the pretty red-blonde hair who sat beside me that you were my brother. She cheered for you almost as hard as I did."

Mary Ellen? Cheering for me? I looked closely at Matty to see if he were teasing me, but there was no way he could know about Mary Ellen. She was my secret, at least at home.

"I told you you'd be great," Mom ruffled my hair, embarrassing me and making Rand smirk as he walked by.

"And, Mike, what a conscientious manager you are, chasing the balls all over the place," she said.

That was the one part of the manager's job Mike had come to hate. If a ball was kicked out of bounds, the manager speedily handed over a replacement ball and raced after the kicked one. It was too much like exercise for his brain to take, Mike said.

Dad turned to Rand and shook his hand. "You did

a fine job, too, young man," Dad said.

"You certainly did," said Mom and beamed one of her megawatt smiles at him.

He blinked and blushed at the compliments, obviously unused to receiving them.

"My mom was going to come today, but she had to work late," he said.

Dad nodded and said, "It'll be nice to meet her now that we know you."

"You boys all ride home with Dad," said Mom. "I'm going to stop at the Pizza Palace and buy us a celebration dinner."

We were all piling into the car when Jeremy and Fonz ran up.

"What time is the canoe trip tomorrow?" Jeremy asked. "Fonz says eleven and I thought you said twelve."

"Eleven, and don't forget your money. You might be Mike's and my guests, but we're not paying for your canoe. We're just going to race you and beat you."

"Don't forget your lunch," Mike said.

"Just promise you won't tip our canoe until after I've eaten." Fonz looked honestly worried. "I'll never survive if my lunch ends up at the bottom of Sedgewick's Run."

"You are such a pig." I said.

"I'm in the middle of a growth spurt," Fonz corrected.

"Don't wear anything you wouldn't want wet," I

yelled out the window as we drove away.

"Who are you going canoeing with?" asked Rand.

"The church youth group," said Mike.

"The church youth group?" Rand said incredulously. I could hear the disbelief and mockery in Rand's voice.

"Would you like to come along?" said Dad. "We'd pick you up at quarter to eleven tomorrow morning."

Rand looked at Dad in surprise. Even though I was gnashing my teeth, I couldn't help noticing how startled he was to be invited. Apparently he didn't get asked to go many places.

"Sounds like it might be fun," he said casually. He shrugged. "Might as well try it. I haven't got anything else to do tomorrow." As he got out of the car, he looked at Mike and me. "It'll be a good way to get to know the guys better." And he laughed nastily.

As soon as Rand closed the car door, Mike and I both jumped on Dad.

"Mr. McCarver, why'd you do that?" asked Mike. "He'll spend all day trying to dunk us."

"Dad, for Pete's sake! He'll ruin the whole trip. Driving him home from practice is more than enough! You don't have to make me put up with him Saturdays, too!"

"Listen, guys," said Dad. "Rand is a lonely kid."

"He's an obnoxious kid," I said unsympathetically.

Dad nodded. "That, too. One canoe trip won't kill you. Besides, you guys were planning to dump each other anyway."

"Yeah, but for fun, not to drown one another."

But we needn't have worried. When we stopped for Rand the next morning, no one at his apartment even answered the door.

7

"Have you ever worked one of these things before?" asked Jeremy. He was holding his canoe paddle in front of him like a baseball bat.

"Obviously you haven't," I said. I held out my paddle. "Like this."

"Next," called Pastor Tony.

"That's us, Mike." I pushed him to the edge of the dock. "You get in the front. I'll take the back."

Jeremy was on my heels. Apparently he'd picked me as his expert. "How do you make them go right or left?" he asked, looking at the canoes.

I bit back an evil grin. "Lean," I said.

"Okay," Jeremy would believe anything.

I stepped into the canoe, trying to look like I knew

what I was doing. In a way I did. I'd gone canoeing lots of times with Mom and Dad and Matty, but I'd never been senior member in the canoe before or canoed with such a herd of people. Also, I'd never canoed in front of Mary Ellen.

When she'd climbed out of Sally Saunders' car, I couldn't believe my luck. Rand hadn't come and Mary Ellen had. Life was good!

The only possible drawback to her presence was that I felt self-conscious. What if I looked like an idiot to her?

Mike's wiggling around trying to figure out what to do made looking good hard. We bobbed and weaved and tilted like a drunken prizefighter.

"Mike, stay still!" Pastor Tony ordered. "No one's allowed to tip until we leave the dock area."

Mike froze.

"Put your paddle in the water on your left," I said. "Stick it in the water and stroke."

Mike pulled four strokes.

"This is hard work!" he yelled, surprised.

I sighed and tried to maneuver through the collection of canoes to Mary Ellen and Sally. I could hear Fonz and Jeremy yelling at each other as they paddled in a circle.

"You take the left side!"

"No, you! I'm not left handed."

"Me neither."

Finally everybody was aboard and fourteen canoes made their erratic way down Sedgewick's

Run. Our first target was a grassy grove thirty minutes away where we'd eat lunch.

By the time we rounded the bend and the first canoes aimed for the bank and lunch, I was finally feeling comfortable. Mike had stopped turning around to ask questions. I'd found a rhythm to my stroking and an ease at angling my paddle in the water to keep us on a straight line. I wasn't feeling smug, just confident.

My paddle bit deeply into the water, and we turned toward the bank. Unfortunately I forgot to look behind me, and suddenly a canoe burst into my peripheral vision, headed right toward us.

Shouts and flailing bodies and a loud *whomp* filled the air.

When I surfaced and blinked the water from my eyes, I saw my canoe bobbing a short distance away, filled with water. Mike was thrashing about doing what he fondly called swimming, aiming for the canoe. Our lunch in its white plastic cooler was floating gently away on the current. At the present rate of travel, it would reach the Atlantic before Mike reached the canoe.

Jeremy and Fonz, dry and snug in their untipped canoe, were laughing so hard they couldn't apologize for dumping us.

"Jase, are you all right?" asked Mary Ellen anxiously.

She and Sally pulled along side of me as I tried not to look as dumb as I felt.

"I'm fine." I smiled what I hoped was a jovial smile. "Wet." I looked at my cooler fast floating downstream. "Lunchless."

Mary Ellen grinned. "You can share ours."

My heart flip-flopped and my smile became real. "Thanks."

"Hang on," said Sally. "We'll tow you to your canoe."

"Just push it to shore," called Pastor Tony as he paddled by. "I'll rescue your lunch."

I began pushing the canoe slowly toward shore. It was heavy with its cargo of water. Mike continued to thrash about as he tried to help.

"Mike, why don't you stop swimming and just stand?" I asked.

"Stand?" Mike stopped beating the water and let his feet sink. He smiled beautifully when they found bottom. He promptly stepped on a mossy rock and went under. He sputtered to the surface and looked daggers at me.

Eager hands reached out and pulled the canoe the last few feet to shore. A couple guys helped me tip it to empty it. We left it tied to a rock as we ate.

Pastor Tony successfully saved our cooler. When I saw what Mary Ellen and Sally had to eat, I was glad he did. Mike and I would never have survived on what the girls would have given us.

As we cleaned up our lunch mess, I whispered to Mike, "Do you think Mary Ellen will canoe with me this afternoon?"

Mike looked horrified. "I hope not! Then I'd have to canoe with Sally. She's a giant! She'd beat me up if I made a mistake!"

"Don't worry," I sighed. "I haven't got the guts to ask her anyway."

We floated along the Run all afternoon. In the shallow spots we got out and ran beside the canoes. In the deep, fast spots we just let the current take us. We had grand water fights, even if Fonz did swing his paddle at the water and get a rock instead.

About 4:30, we piled out of the canoes into waiting cars which took us to Sedgewick's Grove for a wiener roast. A huge bonfire was already going when we arrived.

"This has been one great day!" said Fonz. His T-shirt was ripped, he had a skinned knee, and he owed Sedgewick's Canoe Company fifteen dollars for a broken paddle. "Does your church always do such neat things?"

"It sure does," answered Mike. "We have great times."

"Mike," I said, "you've only been there a few times yourself."

"Yeah. And it's great!"

"Attention, everybody," called Pastor Tony. As everyone looked at him, I stared at Mike. Was church really that important to him?

"After we say grace," said Pastor Tony, "you each can grab a stick from the pile there. Put your hot dog on the end and cook it over the fire. The idea isn't to burn it up but to heat it through. Now let's say grace."

Despite Pastor Tony's warning, Mike and Jeremy burned their hot dogs black. Somehow I never even got the center of mine warm. Everyone agreed that they were delicious.

So were the marshmallows. Only Mary Ellen had the patience necessary to get hers nice and runny and golden brown. The rest of us made torches and ate the resulting carbon balls.

Jeremy ate his seventeenth marshmallow and stuck his stick out in front of him, still smoking.

"Sword fight, McCarver," he yelled at me and lunged.

I jumped back and so did Mary Ellen who was standing next to me. Only her ankle twisted on a small rock and she fell.

For a split second we all froze. Then we all rushed to help Mary Ellen up.

"Hey, I'm sorry," said Jeremy, terribly embarrassed. "Are you okay?"

"I think so," she said as she got up without the help of the hand I had extended. She began to brush herself off when she said a loud, "Ouch!"

She held out her left hand, and there on the tender spot between the thumb and wrist was a cut welling blood.

"Blood!" yelled Mike. "Yuk! I hate blood!"

"Shut up, Mike," I said. "It's no big deal." I grabbed a couple of napkins and pressed them hard against the cut. Mary Ellen's hand felt so small!

"Girls are supposed to be afraid of blood, not guys," said Sally.

"I know," said Mike. "It's dumb, but I hate blood. Mom says I'm just like my dad. He passed out in the delivery room when I was born because he couldn't stand the sight of blood."

"Well, at least they made it to the hospital," said Sally. "I was born in a taxi."

"Were you really?" said Mary Ellen. "I never knew that. I almost didn't make the hospital either because my dad stopped for the entire length of every red light between home and the hospital, even though it was three o'clock in the morning when the streets are deserted. My mom's still mad at him!"

"Well, I almost didn't make it, period," said Jeremy. "I was born early and only weighed four pounds."

"Is that little?" asked Mike.

"That's very little," said Sally.

"I feel left out," said Fonz, looking sad. "I was born just the way you're supposed to be. No one passed out, Mom made it to the hospital, and everything went just right."

I lifted the napkin from Mary Ellen's palm. The bleeding had stopped and she smiled at me. But even her smile couldn't stop my heart from feeling like it was being squeezed in a vise.

All those birth stories! It had just occurred to me. Every kid had a birth story. Every kid but me.

8

Nothing much happened for the next week or so. School and soccer kept on the same as usual. Band did prove to be fun, just as I thought it would, and Mr. Keefer was a great director. I knew he was as impressed with my trumpet playing as Mr. Zindorf was with my soccer. And from where I sat in band, I could watch Mary Ellen play her flute.

The main person who was not impressed with me in any way was Rand. I still had no idea why he disliked me so much, but he certainly did. He continued to make my life miserable in little ways, including talking with Mary Ellen and her friends every day at noon while I watched from afar. Mike, Jeremy, and Fonz enjoyed teasing me about my unrequited love—Mike's term for when you care for someone and they don't like you back.

"Of course," said Fonz very logically, "she has no idea you like her. Maybe we're not talking official unrequited love, just the seventh-grade-shy-kid kind."

The best thing about that time was that Mary Ellen had started coming to the junior high youth group with Sally. She said she wanted to come all the time. Although not quite as enthusiastic as Mike, she seemed to have a good time and certainly listened when Pastor Tony talked.

Lots of the things Pastor Tony said weren't new to me. I had been going to church all my life. But they were new to Mike, and he was funny in his enthusiasm.

"Not only is God with me everywhere," he told Mom and Dad one night on the way home, "He knows exactly what I feel and He'll give me strength to handle anything I face."

"That means a lot to you, Mike?" asked Dad.

"If you lived at my house, Mr. McCarver," he answered very seriously, "you'd understand."

The next youth group activity coming up was a bowling party. I'd only bowled once in my life, Mike had never bowled at all, but we were going. Jeremy and Fonz wanted to come too, and Pastor Tony said it was fine.

Then one Thursday night at dinner, Matty

brought up a subject I'd been sort of trying to forget.

"Hey, do you all realize that Heritage Day is a week from tomorrow, and we still haven't heard from the adoption agency?"

"It's been a month since I wrote. We should hear soon," said Mom. "But just in case, you'd better plan an alternative costume."

"You can wear my kilt," said Dad.

I laughed and Matty said, "Dad, you're six feet tall. There's no way I could wear your kilt. It'd drag on the ground."

"How about mine?" offered Mom. "I'm much shorter."

"Mom. Dad." Matty looked pained. "No skirt."

"Prince Charles is always photographed in his kilt," said Dad.

"That's because people would never make fun of a prince, but people would love to make fun of a little redheaded kid in a skirt. I think I'll go as an early American thief."

"We Gardiniers would be very proud to have you represent us," said Mom.

"Don't think Scotland won't get any attention, Dad," said Matty. "There's going to be Scottish dancers and Polish dancers, a Chinese restaurant is going to make us all some food, a French teacher is going to teach us a French song, we're going to see a movie from Africa, and all kinds of other stuff."

Dad looked impressed. "Maybe I'll wear my kilt and come."

The next day, after lunch I was walking down the hall behind Mary Ellen as Rand walked her to class. I couldn't help hearing their conversation.

"Come on, Mary Ellen. It's Friday night. We could have a great time."

"I'm sorry, Rand. I'm not allowed to go out on single dates."

My eyebrows went up. Had her parents gone to the same parenting school as mine?

"Besides," Mary Ellen continued. "I'm already busy tonight."

"Somebody else? Come on. I'd show you a better time, and you know it."

I didn't gag, but I felt like it.

"I'm going bowling tonight," she said as she stopped outside the science room door. She turned to enter and saw me behind her. "Jase is going too, and Mike and Sally and Jeremy and Fonz and a whole bunch of kids."

Rand glared at me. "Jase? You're going bowling with Jase?"

I smiled sweetly at his surprised and angry look, tried not to look smug, and said, "Seven, Mary Ellen?"

She nodded and walked into the room. I followed quickly before Rand could lay a hand on me. I slid into my seat contentedly recalling Rand's dismay at the thought of Mary Ellen going somewhere with me. He'd obviously not even heard her say Mike and Sally and Jeremy and Fonz. Just me. I grinned. Too bad it wasn't just me. Though if it was just me, I'd never take her bowling, not the way I bowled.

A hand touched mine. It was Judy Post.

"What?" I asked happily. It was the first time I'd smiled at her since she'd called me a reject, and she looked surprised.

"Over there," she said, pointing to the door.

I looked at the door and my grin froze on my face. Rand stood there with a clenched fist raised, and he was waving it at me.

9

"Hey, shrimp!"

I looked up from my gym locker. Rand was standing in the aisle at the opening of the alcove of lockers I shared with Mike and Jeremy and Fonz. He was so big he practically blotted out the light.

I couldn't help wishing I hadn't stopped to talk with Mr. Keefer about band. Since I was a bit late, the other guys had already gone out to practice. It was just Rand and me.

"Shrimp?" I looked around as if I didn't know what he meant. "I don't see any seafood here."

"Funny," said Rand. He had an ugly sneer on his handsome face. "You are not going out with Mary Ellen tonight."

"Sure I am," I said over my hammering heart. "I'm going out with her and Sally and Mike and Fonz and Jeremy and a bunch of other kids."

"Huh?"

"The youth group at church is going. Remember when we went canoeing?"

"That's when you went in the drink, isn't it?" Scorn dripped from his tongue like ice cream from a cone on a hot summer day.

Stung by his attitude I said hotly, "Didn't you ever tip a canoe?"

As soon as I spoke, I had a sudden flash of insight, and I knew he'd never even been in a canoe. I realized that he never had the opportunity to do many things that I thought were a normal part of life.

Be careful, I warned myself. You might begin to feel the teensiest bit sorry for him.

"Tip a canoe? Not me," Rand said, bragging. "I'm better than that."

Sure, I thought. Sure.

"Look, Rand, don't you think trading insults is a bit dumb?" I tried to look my most sincere. Inside I was a nervous wreck. "Let's just go play soccer and leave the name calling behind." I pushed my locker shut and began walking toward him. I had no idea what I'd do if he didn't move before I got to him. Scream maybe.

He didn't budge until I was almost touching him. Then he fell back and began walking just behind me. He swung his hand out and began flicking my one ear while at the same time he walked on my heel.

Because I didn't know what else to do, I ran ahead, threw the locker room door open and hurried outside to people.

"You are a jerk, Purcell," I yelled as I joined the team in the middle of a lap around the field. "A real jerk!"

He merely grinned.

Once Rand was safely in goal, practice went well. Our big game with Edison Junior High was next Friday. It wasn't our last game, but it was our biggest rivalry. Edison was the other junior high in town, and it looked like we could take them. Mr. Zindorf told me I'd be starting center forward if I kept up the good work.

"Congratulations, Jase!" said Mom at dinner when I told the family. "I knew you could do it."

"Great!" said Dad, reaching over to shake my hand.

"Is that Rand guy starting too?" asked Matty, red curls bouncing.

"Yeah, he's starting in goal. At least he can't push me around when he's stuck there."

"If he gives you so much trouble, Jase," said Matty, "why don't you pop him one?"

"Are you kidding?" Even the suggestion made me sweat. "You've seen how big he is!"

"Fighting's not the answer anyway," said Mom.

"Christians don't handle conflict that way. Jase will think of something."

"I know he's a real problem, Jase," said Dad. "Just hang in there. It'll take care of itself in time."

Yeah. Maybe by the time I'm one hundred. But I kept my doubts to myself and changed the subject to my other big news.

"I also found out that I made first chair trumpet today," I announced, waiting to see their reaction.

"You did?" Mom was surprised.

"I told you I would," I said.

"You beat out the ninth grade guys and the girl with the lipstick?" Matty asked.

"The girl with the lipstick was my hardest competition. She's really good. She took out a tissue, wiped some awful purple-pink stuff off and blew. Her trouble is timing. She can't keep it."

"So you were better," said Matty.

I grinned. "I was better."

"And Rand's not in band?"

"Rand's not in band."

"Congratulations again, Jase," said Dad. "It's about time the McCarvers had a musician."

"No others?" asked Matty.

"None," said Dad. "Athletes, hunters, fishermen, even a bowler or two, but no musicians. Except for you two."

"I'm not a musician," Matty said. "I'm learning to play the clarinet at school, but I'm only doing it because it gets me out of class one hour a week.

Besides, I want to go on those neat band trips when I'm in high school."

"Dad." I cleared my throat hesitantly. "Mr. Keefer said I should take private lessons. He said there's a man he knows who could really teach me how to play the trumpet."

"Private lessons?" Dad looked surprised and unenthusiastic, just like I knew he would. "I don't know, Jase. I suppose you still want a piano, too?"

I nodded. I'd wanted a piano for at least two years, not a new one, just a secondhand one. I just couldn't convince Dad no matter how hard I tried. He couldn't imagine anyone wanting a piano. Pianos got left to you by wealthy old aunts. You certainly didn't spend good money for them.

"We ought to consider it, Hal," said Mom. "Just because we don't play an instrument doesn't mean Jase shouldn't."

Back in fifth grade I'd started taking trumpet lessons at school because Mom thought it would be good for me. It would make me more "well-rounded." The lessons were free, except for the secondhand trumpet which Dad bought under protest.

It was a great surprise to all of us that I seemed to know almost automatically how to read music and play. And most surprising of all was that I had fun doing it. It was like a door had opened into this marvelous amusement park that I hadn't known was there, and I could go in and play whenever I wanted.

Mom and Dad were proud when I had solos in the school concerts, but they didn't really hear Mrs. Paton, my then music teacher, when she told them she felt I was musically gifted.

"He should have private lessons, Mr. McCarver," she told Dad after the sixth grade spring concert. I'd just played what Mrs. Paton and I knew was a pretty complex song for a kid my age but Dad didn't. He just knew I hadn't made any great mistakes.

"He should have piano, too," she said.

Dad had stared at me back then just like he was staring at me now, over the rim of his coffee cup. I tried not to squirm, but I felt like yelling, "It's okay to like music!" I often wondered what Dad would say if I told him that sometimes I liked music better than sports.

I escaped from the table as soon as possible. Even in my room, I could still feel Dad eyeing me over that cup as if I was some biology specimen he'd never seen before and couldn't quite believe existed.

What did he think I was, some sort of freak because I liked music as well as sports? Because I was different from the hunting-fishing-bowling McCarver sportsmen? Because I was adopted?

I slammed my bedroom door because it felt good and because I knew it made Dad angry. I threw myself on my bed and stared at the ceiling. Even Petey's chirps couldn't cheer me.

My real parents would have understood about the music and gotten me lessons and a piano.

The whole problem was the adoption. I hated it! It wasn't a white-hot fiery hate that made me want to beat people up or break things, at least not usually. It was a slow-cooking hatred that made me resentful and angry.

"God," I said to the ceiling, "if You're with us everywhere like Pastor Tony keeps telling us, then why weren't You with me when I was born? Why didn't You make my mother keep me so I'd feel I belonged? You could have kept me from being a reject . . . and You didn't."

Suddenly the door to my room opened and Mike fell in. I was busy being grouchy and nasty. I didn't want to be disturbed.

"What do you want?" I was not polite. Then I noticed that he was so upset he was shaking.

"What's wrong with you?" he asked. My sharp words had surprised and hurt him.

"I hate it, Mike. I hate it! I hate it!"

Mike looked bewildered. "Hate what?"

"Being adopted! It's terrible! It's the worst thing that can happen to a person! I don't belong anywhere! I've got this big hole in my life, and I don't know how to plug it up!" I punched my pillow like it was responsible.

"You've got holes?" Mike cried, his voice quivering. "You think you've got troubles? Hah!"

Mike's distress finally cut through my own hurt. I sat up and stared at him.

His eyes were red like he'd been crying and his

hair was all wild.

"You don't know bad, Jase." He began to cry, big silent tears pouring down his face. "You don't know holes. I'm so full of holes from all their fighting that I feel like I'm bleeding to death."

I didn't need to ask who *they* were. His mom and dad must be at it again.

He pulled his glasses off and stuffed them in his jeans pocket. He wiped at his tears with his T-shirt, but they kept falling.

I didn't know what to do. How do you tell your friend that it's okay when you both know it's not?

"Are they fighting now?" I finally asked.

He nodded. "They started at dinner when Mom burned the meat because Dad was late. Next thing I knew, they were screaming and swearing and then Mom grabbed a plate and threw it at him. It missed and bounced off the wall. Gravy was just running down the wall to the floor."

I couldn't imagine people throwing things at each other. When Mom got mad at Dad, she said in a real stern voice, "Harold, we must talk." And Dad knew he was in trouble.

The only time that I knew of that he'd yelled at her was one night when she left the headlights on and the car battery was dead the next morning.

"Ellie," he yelled as he stood there in his gray pin-striped suit with his briefcase in his hand, "how could you be so stupid?"

Mom, in her fuzzy pink robe, looked at him,

drew herself up tall and said in a voice dripping icicles, "I beg your pardon, Harold."

I never could figure out if she was apologizing for the lights or reprimanding him for his tone of voice. Probably both.

But throwing things?

Mike grabbed my pillow and buried his face in it.

"He was packing his suitcase when I left," his muffled voice told me. "She stood in the doorway saying, 'Mike, tell him his socks are in the second drawer.' Then he'd say, 'Mike, tell her I can take care of myself.' 'Mike, tell him . . .' 'Mike, tell her . . .' I hate it when they talk through me!"

"Will he actually leave?" I asked. Sometimes I wondered if that wouldn't be better. Then Mike wouldn't live in the middle of a war zone.

Mike lowered the pillow. "I don't think so. They're playing some kind of sick game about the house. Neither wants the other guy to get it, so neither will leave. They seem to get some weird pleasure out of hurting each other."

Again I was silent. After a time I asked, "You want to spend the night here?"

"Can I?" said Mike. "I'd much rather God helped me through this here than there."

Mom took one look at Mike's face and repeated my invitation to him. She even offered to call Mike's mom who apparently stopped fighting long enough to answer the phone.

Dad drove us to the bowling alley. Though

neither Mike nor I felt much like bowling, it was better than staying home. When we climbed out of the car, Dad looked at Mike.

"Mike," he said, "I want you to know you're always welcome at our home, and we're glad you're Jase's friend."

I thought Mike would start to cry again.

10

Bowling did a lot to take our minds off our troubles. Rarely have so few been so bad at something nonacademic.

Jeremy kept throwing the ball rather than rolling it. Every time he took his turn, there was a terrible WHAP! as the ball hit the alley about a third of the way down.

Fonz had gotten a ball so heavy he could hardly lift it without it falling off his fingers. Because of the weight, there was no way he could control the thing, and every turn at least one of his throws went down the gutter.

Mike couldn't get his feet to coordinate with his hands, so he always rolled with his feet all tangled up and his balance all haywire. No one was more surprised than he when he made a strike in the fifth frame.

I wasn't much better. In trying to look like Joe Pro, I developed a backward swing that was great. The problem was that the finger holes in my ball were so large that one time the ball slipped right off in the middle of my backswing. It landed with a crash behind me, missing Mike's foot by an inch.

I thought my "friends" would never stop laughing. And even Mary Ellen and Sally and two other girls on the next lane seemed to find humor in my poor form. I was able to redeem myself by knocking all the pins down on my next roll.

"Strike!" I yelled, jumping up and down.

"Spare," said Mike. "The one you dropped behind you was your first ball. This is your second. All the pins knocked over in two shots is a spare."

"You can't count that backward bounce as a turn!" I said. "The ball's got to go forward to count as a turn."

Mike just grinned wickedly.

"They should thank us," said Jeremy after the first game ended. "They haven't had such clean gutters in years."

"Final scores: Jeremy, 70; Fonz 45; Mike 85; me, 95," I announced.

Terrible scores all, but at least I'd won. The only thing that ruined my sense of accomplishment was Mary Ellen's score—115.

She grinned at me happily. "I hope I do better next time," she said.

"Have you bowled much?" I asked suspiciously.

"Never before," she said. "I just aim and roll."

I snorted. "Then that was just beginner's luck. We'll see who wins this next game."

She did, and quite handily. She had this run of strikes, five in a row.

"When I'm finally allowed to date, Mike," I said as we waited for Mom and Dad to pick us up, "remind me never to take Mary Ellen bowling. Ever."

We were sitting on the steps of the Bowling Arena. Mike grinned at me, the lights bouncing off his glasses, making his eyes disappear. He looked like a weird insect.

Everyone was gone but us. Mom and Dad had gone to the mall down in Valley Green, about forty-five minutes away, and we knew we'd probably have to wait a while for them.

We sat in silence for a few minutes. Then I said, "Feeling better than you were when you came over this evening?"

Mike nodded. "When I'm around other people, home seems like a foreign planet. Laughing and fooling around help the hurt to go away, at least for a while. How are you feeling?"

I shrugged. "Okay, I guess. Though I'd feel even better if I'd beaten Mary Ellen."

A car pulled up in front of us.

"Still waiting for your ride?" It was Pastor Tony.

"They went to Valley Green Mall. They'll be here soon."

"I'll wait with you," he said. "Let me go park."

Pastor Tony took a seat on the steps next to Mike.

"How's school going this year?" he asked.

Typical adult question, but Pastor Tony seemed as though he really wanted to know. Next thing I knew, we were telling him about Rand.

"Have you been able to figure out why he picks on you so much, Jase?" Pastor Tony asked.

"Because he's a jerk," I said.

Pastor Tony laughed. "I think there's more to it than that."

"I don't know what," I said. "He's tall and good looking and the girls like him and he plays great soccer."

"How about academically?"

"Mediocre," said Mike.

"So that's one possible reason. How about his family?" asked Pastor Tony.

"Not so good," I said.

"Worse than mine," said Mike.

"You've trouble at home, Mike?" said Pastor Tony. "I don't know you well yet, so I don't know about your family. Will you tell me?"

"They hate each other," he said.

Pastor Tony looked surprised. "Who hates each other?"

"My mom and dad."

"Why do you think that?"

"Because they tell each other so all the time." Mike's face had resumed its distressed look.

Pastor Tony shook his head sympathetically. "Tough situation."

"Very," I said. "Tonight his father said he was leaving."

"But I don't think he will," said Mike quickly. "It's just a weapon he likes to use."

"Families can hurt each other very badly." said Pastor Tony. "And often it's the kids who get hurt worst of all."

"Sometimes I look at my parents, especially when they're fighting, and I feel like I don't really belong in this family," said Mike. "It's like they're strangers I never saw before, strangers I don't even want to know."

"I feel that way about my family, too," I said. "They're just people who are there to complicate my life, not people I know and care about."

Pastor Tony nodded. "That's typical of how teenagers feel. I've found that it's not just kids in troubled homes like yours, Mike, or adopted kids, Jase. It seems to be all teenagers, and it's part of getting you ready to leave home in a few more years."

"It's funny," said Mike. "Here I am in my real family, and all I ever see is anger. And here Jase is in an adopted family, and all he sees is kindness and love. It's enough to make me put myself up for adoption."

Pastor Tony smiled. "One of the most difficult

things about growing up is coming to terms with the things in our lives that don't seem fair. We ask ourselves why God didn't make everything fine and good—the way we want it."

I looked at Pastor Tony. That was exactly what I wondered all the time. Why had God let my mom give me up? Why did He let Mike's parents fight so much and hurt Mike? I even wondered why Rand's mom ignored him.

"Well, why doesn't He make things fair?" asked Mike. "It seems to me that He's given me an extra large dose of trouble."

Pastor Tony nodded. "I just want to ask you one question, Mike. Does God make mistakes?"

Mike shook his head. "He can't make mistakes. He's God."

"Okay," said Pastor Tony. "Then He didn't make a mistake having you born into your family even though He knew they were going to fight all the time. He didn't make a mistake having Jase adopted either."

"Sometimes I wonder," I said.

Pastor Tony nodded. "I know what you mean. I don't understand a lot of things either. That's where faith comes in. We have the confidence in God that He knows what's going on even if we don't."

"Does He ever promise to take the bad situations away?" asked Mike.

Pastor Tony shook his head. "Nope. He just promises to be with us through the bad times."

A car pulled up beside us.

"Do I see a pair of lost kids who need a ride?" asked Dad.

We said good-bye to Pastor Tony, climbed in, and spent the next few minutes admiring Matty's new sneakers.

"But you can't wear them on Heritage Day," I said. "Too good looking."

Matty grinned happily.

Suddenly Dad hit the brakes and pulled off the road.

"Whatever's wrong, Hal?" asked Mom who had been watching us in the back seat.

"Dad? What happened?" I asked.

Dad opened his door and climbed out.

"Rand? Is that you?" he called into the darkness.

Rand? Walking along the dark road at eleven at night? Alone?

"Move over, guys," Dad said to us. "Make room for Rand."

I opened the car door and slid over to make room for my favorite person.

Rand, wearing jeans and a T-shirt and goose-bumps, sat beside me. He stared straight ahead.

"Are you going home?" asked Dad as he started the car.

"No!" Rand all but shouted.

We all started in surprise and he quieted his voice.

"No. Could you drop me at my grandparents' farm?"

"You're not running away, are you, Rand?" asked Dad. "I don't want to do something that will make your mother worry."

"No, I'm not running away. But she'll never know I'm gone anyway. She dropped me at the movies at seven and was supposed to pick me up at nine. She never showed. After an hour and a half I got tired of waiting and started walking."

"Do you think she has car trouble or something?" Mom asked. "Should we go check at your house?"

Rand snorted. "She was with Adam when she dropped me off. He's one of her boyfriends. She's just forgotten me, not for the first time."

I didn't dare watch Rand because I don't think he realized how hurt his voice sounded. I didn't want him to see that I felt badly for him. I might get frustrated and angry at Mom and Dad, but I don't know what I'd do if all of a sudden they stopped taking me places and things.

I should have saved my sympathy.

Rand turned to me just as we reached the farm and said as nastily and quietly as he could, "I thought you were going bowling with Mary Ellen. She stand you up, and all you had left was a cozy night with Mommy and Daddy?"

11

Monday night after dinner Mom pushed her chair back from the table.

"Stay put, guys. I've got to get something."

She returned in a few minutes with a 9 x 12 envelope that had been opened. My stomach dropped when I saw the return address—Bedlow County Adoption Agency.

"Hey, our adoption stuff," said Matty, all excited and enthused. "What's it say? Am I really a prince with a huge kingdom in some rare place like Tibet? Or is my father a millionaire who's set up this big trust fund for me when I'm eighteen?"

Mom and Dad laughed.

"I'm afraid not, Matty," said Mom. "Your mom

was a high school junior who wanted to become an elementary school teacher. She was sixteen and had—get this—red hair and blue eyes."

Matty grinned.

Mom continued. "She's from a Scots-Irish background, was 5′ 6″ tall, and weighed 115 pounds. She had a part-time job at McDonald's, and she has a brother and two sisters."

"I've got an uncle and two aunts," said Matty.

"Your mom played hockey, ran track, and liked to read. She went to church and Sunday school and she wore braces for two years."

Matty ran his tongue over his teeth. "Do you think I'll need braces?" He clenched his teeth and spread his lips. "They're straight enough, aren't they?" he said in a garbled voice.

"They're great, dear," said Mom automatically. She cleared her throat nervously. "Matty, I don't have very much to tell you about your father. For some reason, there's not much here."

"Don't worry about it," Matty said. "It doesn't bother me. Just tell me all you've got."

"He was a high school senior, had brown hair and hazel eyes, and was tall."

"Tall?" Matty's eyes sparkled. "How tall? Does that mean I'll be tall?"

Mom looked at the paper again. "It doesn't say how tall, but it sounds like you've probably got a chance to be near six feet."

Matty nodded happily. Lucky stiff.

"What's his nationality?' the kid asked, obviously thinking of Heritage Day.

"It doesn't say."

"And my mother was Scots-Irish?"

Mom nodded.

"Then I'm going to go as an early American Gardinier chicken thief. No offense, Dad."

Dad, who is a very practical man, understood. No skirts.

"Now, Jase," said Mom.

I took a deep breath. "Go ahead," I said. "I can take it."

"It's not that bad, honey. Not at all."

I was unconvinced.

"Your mom was twenty-one, a college honors graduate who had majored in music. Her specialty was keyboard."

No wonder I want a piano, I thought.

"She had brown hair and eyes, was 5′ 5″, and weighed 130. She was in good health but had mononucleosis when she was a college freshman. She was going to graduate school in New York City the fall after you were born and wanted a career performing on the concert stage."

"Maybe she'll be famous some day, Jase, and you'll meet her," said Matty.

Maybe she was famous already. With my lack of knowledge about the concert stage, I'd never know it.

"Your father was twenty-two and had graduated

from the same college as your mother. He was a business major with an interest in international banking. He was going to graduate school, too, in Philadelphia. He was 5′ 10″, weighed 160 pounds, and played soccer and lacrosse all through college."

It was weird hearing about people I didn't know but who had at least partly made me what I was.

Mom continued. "Apparently they had gone together for two years and talked about getting married. It was their different career goals that caused them to breakup."

"5′ 10″ isn't bad, Jase," said Matty.

I shrugged. "Can I see the sheet, Mom?"

"Sure." She handed me a paper with lots of typing on it. I read through it quickly. It said essentially what she'd told me plus some stuff about their health and my natural grandparents.

"Do you think you have enough information there for your genetics report?" Dad asked.

"I don't know," I said. "I've got to think about it for awhile. I know one girl who told Mr. Freneau that she's had a stepfather since she was three, and things are so bad between her mother and her real father that she can't even ask her mom about him. Mr. Freneau told her to write a report on Gregory Mendel, the father of genetics, instead."

"So he's obviously willing to help out those who, like you, are in awkward positions," Dad said.

Awkward positions. What an understatement.

"Wait, Jase," said Mom as I started to leave the

table. "I have one more thing."

She stopped and we all looked at her.

Uncertain of how to proceed, she reached in the folder and pulled out a sealed, letter-sized envelope and stared at it for a minute. Then, looking at Matty she said, "Matthew, I don't want you to get upset, okay?"

"Okay," he said. "About what?"

"Jase, this letter is for you. It's from your birth mother. Apparently she sent it to the agency shortly after we got you. They've had it all this time and weren't willing or able to pass it on to us until I wrote asking for any information available about you two."

I stared at the letter like it was alive. I was eager to know what it said and I was frightened. What if my mother was a wonderful person? What if she was terrible? If I read that letter, I'd know. It seemed safer to imagine.

"I know, Jase," said Mom, "that you have very mixed feelings about being adopted. So I give this to you with some fear. Dad and I don't want you to be hurt, but we think you deserve to hear what she has to say."

She extended the letter and I reached for it. I could hardly breathe. Everyone seemed to be holding their breath, too.

I slit the envelope and pulled out a piece of paper folded in thirds. I opened it slowly.

My dear son, it began.

I refolded it quickly and looked up to find everyone staring at me.

"Can I go read this in my room?" I asked. My voice didn't squeak too much.

"Sure, son. Go ahead." Dad smiled and nodded.

I sat on the edge of my bed with Petey on my shoulder. I unfolded the letter and began reading.

My dear son,

I called you Patrick after your grandfather, my father, and I often wonder what your new parents have named you.

I feel a strong need to tell you I love you and think of you all the time.

I want you to know that I did not give you up because of any problem in you. You were perfect, as cute as could be. When I held you in the hospital, nursed and changed you, I was filled with delight at how wonderful you were.

I know you will wonder why I gave you up. I made all my choices based on what I felt would make your life happiest.

It's a funny thing, but having a baby when you're not married is a situation in which there are no "right" answers. If I kept you, there would be problems. If I let you go, there would be problems. Where, I asked myself over and over, were the least problems for you.

I believed—and still believe—that adoption gave you a better head start than any other possibility.

I want you to know that your natural father is a

fine and talented man. I'd be happy if you grew up to be like him.

Well, Patrick, I grieve deeply that I won't be able to hear your first word or see your first step or take you to Sunday school or music lessons or Little League. I have this hole in my life that I know will always be there because you aren't. I pray every day for you and the family you are now a part of. They are so fortunate to have you—and you to have them. Love them, Patrick, and always know I love you.

I lay back on the bed and stared at the ceiling. She had a hole in her life. Whoever she was, she had a hole, too. Somehow that made me feel better. She sounded nice and said my father was nice.

Petey walked up and down my chest as I tried to sort out how I felt. Did I hate her? Did I love her? Did I feel anything toward her?

Petey pecked me on the chin. I ruffled his feathers and laughed as he climbed up on my chin, across my cheek and sat on my forehead.

She had holes and I had holes, and somehow Petey was more real than she was.

12

Rand was acting more rottenly than ever. I figured it was because he was upset about Friday.

By now he knew that I had been bowling in the same group as Mary Ellen. He even knew we had bowled on adjoining lanes. While I wished that meant something significant, I knew it didn't. Rand wasn't dumb; he must have known, too. He just chose to make it an issue. Probably he thought that if he kept at me, I'd be too distracted to bring up his flight to his grandparents.

Tuesday after practice we were waiting for Dad. Mike and I were standing together when Rand came out. Most of the other kids had already been picked up.

Suddenly something bounced off my head.

"What?" I reached up, and at the same time Mike jumped.

Rand giggled and continued entertaining himself by raining pebbles on Mike and me. We tried to ignore him, but it was difficult when it felt like BBs bouncing on our brains.

"Purcell, cut it out!" I ordered when a particularly large pebble ricocheted off my skull.

"What's the matter, Jase?" he asked in his silky, sulky voice. "Afraid you might bruise?"

"Why don't you find another way home and get out of my life?" I yelled. "You are nothing but trouble!"

Rand grinned. "But your father is so nice. I wouldn't want to hurt his feelings by turning down the ride."

"Believe me," I said, "he'd survive without you."

"You know," said Rand with a wide-eyed, innocent look that meant he was about to get nasty. "It's hard to believe that you're related to that nice man. Oh—" He drew a quick breath. "I just remembered. You're not related, are you? You're a reject."

If he meant to hurt me, I realized with surprise that somehow it hadn't worked. I had done a lot of thinking since Judy Post yelled at me on the bus.

But he did make me furious! What right did he have to make fun of me, especially considering his private life? The only thing that kept me from saying something nasty back was Judy Post's face in my memory, and the fact that I couldn't think of anything clever to say.

"You know, Rand," said Mike quietly. "Jase may be adopted, but of the three of us, his father is the only one who cares enough to pick him up after practice."

Rand looked like he had been suddenly bitten by a poisonous snake, and bitten where it hurt. He turned his back and stalked away, leaving us alone until Dad came.

Wednesday, he was at it again.

"Hey, Midget," he called as soon as we came out of the locker room after practice.

Somehow I knew he didn't mean Mike even though Mike is shorter than I am.

I pretended I hadn't heard anything.

"Hey, Midget," he repeated as he walked up to me and planted a huge finger in my chest. "I wrote a song for you."

With a smirk he looked at the other guys who were still waiting for their rides and began reciting in a sing-song voice:

"You'd think the reject
Would suspect
That his lady doesn't care.

"You'd think the reject
Would suspect
That he hasn't got a prayer.

"You'd think the reject
Would suspect
That they'll never make a pair.

"But he doesn't
'Cause he's dumb
And his head is full of air."

There was this small, unbelieving silence as we all stared at him. I personally wanted to shrink him to ant size and squish him.

Then Mike spoke in a quiet, wondering tone. "Hey, Rand, you are very courageous to sing a song like that about yourself. But I don't think you should call yourself a reject. After all, Mr. Zindorf likes you."

Everybody started to laugh and Rand turned scarlet. He began to sputter, but before he could think of a retort, Dad arrived.

"I'm afraid to see what he's got planned for tomorrow," I told everybody at dinner. "Whatever it is, I know I'll be the target, and so will Mike if he's not careful."

"You know he's jealous, don't you, Jase?" said Mom.

"I guess so," I said uncertainly. "But why?"

"I think it's us," said Dad. "It started over soccer, but now it's us."

"Us?"

"The family," Dad said. "It's bad enough that you

do well academically and play a mean game of soccer and think the same girl is cute. But, you have the backing at home that he can only dream of."

I looked skeptical. "I don't know, Dad. Rand doesn't need a family. He's as close to independent as any kid I know."

"And believe me," said Dad, "that's his problem."

I went to my room to do Mrs. Stevens' dumb vocabulary book and to start reading a book for a book report. Instead, Petey and I reread the letter from my birth mom.

"Stop eating the letter," I said to the bird as he nibbled daintily at the one edge of the paper.

He tilted his head and chirped, then went back to making tiny triangular holes just as he pleased.

All at once I wanted Mom and Dad to read the letter. I knew it would make them feel good. And knowing Mom, she must have been biting her tongue for the last two days. She who wants-to-know-everything never asked me about the letter.

I was just outside the living room when I heard my name and realized Mom and Dad were talking about me.

"Private lessons for Jase, Ellie? Buy a piano? For a thirteen-year-old?"

"You know what the information from the adoption agency indicated, Hal. Genetically, he's musical."

"But you know how fast kids change their minds."

"You'd give him tennis lessons if he wanted them, wouldn't you?" Mom asked. "Or get him ski equipment? Secondhand, of course."

"But you can use sports all your life," Dad said. "People are physically active even with gray hair, or they watch them, which is almost as much fun. What do you do with music?"

"Play it, Hal. Sing it. Listen to it. People use music all their lives, too."

"I guess," Dad said doubtfully. "I just can't imagine wanting to play music on purpose."

Mom laughed. "You just remember when your mother made you take piano lessons from your next-door neighbor."

"I hated it," said Dad. "It gave me a nervous tic under my right eye."

"Everyone doesn't hate music, Hal. Just turn on the radio, and you hear all kinds of people making all kinds of music. And all kinds of people listen to it by the hour."

Dad grunted. "What if he wants to be a musician?"

"For a career? You want him to be a professional soccer player instead? One's about as unstable as the other."

"At least I understand wanting to be a sports star," Dad said. "I used to dream that myself."

They were silent for a moment.

Finally Mom spoke. "If he's got talent, Hal, we've got to give him the opportunity to develop it."

"I know." Dad sighed. "It's just hard to handle these genetic differences. Since there's no guideline whatsoever with Jase or with Matty, I feel blindfolded sometimes. I can't see where I'm going, and I can't decide which direction I should take."

Dad must have stood up because I could hear him pacing.

He continued: "Jase didn't get his musical ability or his keen mind or even his sports ability from the McCarvers and the Gardiniers. He gets them from somebody we never knew."

Dad sat. "Ellie, half the time I don't understand how he thinks. He's smarter than I am, may he never find out. And, Matty. Where'd he get that marvelous personality? He can talk to anybody."

"God gave them those genes, Hal. We knew when we got them that they wouldn't be McCarvers and Gardiniers, but we also knew we wanted a chance to mold them by McCarver and Gardinier values. We wanted to be parents. God just gave us an extraordinary pair."

"Does Jase play soccer just to make me happy?" Dad asked suddenly.

"I don't think so, dear. He seems to like it. And obviously Matty loves football and baseball."

"What if Jase decides not to play sports any more?"

"What if he does?"

Dad sighed again. "Will you call that Mr. Keefer and get his friend's name and number?"

"And check the want-ads for a used piano?"

"Sure. Check. But no guarantees."

"You're a good father, Hal. You know there are lots of birth children who are totally different from their parents."

"But at least there's Great Uncle Joe or somebody that the kid resembles."

I heard the sound of a kiss and I slipped back to my room.

Petey and I lay on my bed. He pecked happily at the button on my shirt while I thought. I had never realized before that not being McCarver/Gardinier-born had made me a puzzle to my parents.

I had holes. My birth mother had holes. How strange to realize that Mom and Dad had holes, too.

13

"Here, Jase. I was asked to give this to you."

Judy Post stood by my desk in Mr. Freneau's room Thursday after lunch and held a note out to me.

"Thanks, Judy." I took the note and opened it.

> *Jase—*
>
> *I need to see you for a few minutes after school. Please stop by my room.*
>
> *Mr. Keefer*

I folded the paper and stared at it. Did Mr. Keefer want to see me about arranging private lessons? Much as I wanted them, today wasn't a good day to talk about it. In fact, this whole week wasn't good with the big game coming up. I didn't want to do anything to make Mr. Zindorf mad at me because I wanted to start, and he hated lateness. I wished I could write back to Mr. Keefer and say, "Let's make it some morning instead."

I shrugged. I had no choice but to go see Mr. Keefer.

I passed the note to Mike. "Explain to Mr. Z. for me?"

He nodded.

Mr. Freneau came into the room and I walked up to his desk. I had thought a lot about what I was about to ask him, but I was still nervous.

"Mr. Freneau?"

"Jason. What can I do for you?"

"It's about those genetics reports."

"Problems?"

"Awkward problems," I said. "See, I'm adopted and I don't know much about my birth family."

Mr. Freneau nodded. "Don't worry about it. Just do a written report on Gregory Mendel, the father of genetics."

I made a face. "Somehow fruitflies don't interest me very much, Mr. Freneau. But I have another idea. Can I write about how strange it is to have traits from two families? I know a little about my birth parents, and I know a lot about my real parents and how they've tried to raise me and my brother."

"You want to write about being the product of two families?" Mr. Freneau seemed surprised.

Apparently no one had ever asked him if they could do that before.

"Yeah," I said, feeling a little unsure of myself. "You know the old argument—is it your genes or your training that makes you what you are?"

Mr. Freneau smiled broadly, and I began to breathe again. He seemed to like the idea.

"Sounds like a very clever way to handle the situation, Jason. I'll be looking forward to what you say."

Weak with relief, I made my way to my seat. As I passed Mary Ellen's desk, she reached out and touched my arm.

"I was listening, Jase," she whispered. "I just want you to know I think it's neat you're adopted."

"You do?"

She nodded. "It makes you special somehow."

The thrill of victory! Mary Ellen thought I was special! Surely that was worth a few holes?

After school I hurried to Mr. Keefer's room. The sooner I got there, the sooner I could get to soccer.

"Mr. Keefer?" I looked around, but the band director wasn't there. Great. I slouched in a chair and waited for him to show up. Five minutes passed. Ten minutes.

Just when I decided he'd forgotten, I saw Mrs. Adams, the vocal music teacher, walk by the door deep in conversation with Mrs. Stevens. I ran out the door. Mrs. Adams would know where Mr. Keefer was.

"Mrs. Adams?" I called.

She stopped, looked at me and smiled absently. Mrs. Stevens kept talking and Mrs. Adams kept listening. She held up a finger like I was supposed to wait a minute. I waited.

Suddenly the two of them began laughing like Judy Post and her dorky friends. I rolled my eyes. Their I-don't-believe-its and it's-the-truths lasted forever. I bit the inside of my mouth and waited.

Finally Mrs. Adams looked at me and actually saw me.

"What can I do for you, Jase?"

"I'm supposed to meet Mr. Keefer. Do you know where he is?"

"Mr. Keefer? There must be some mistake. He leaves right after his last class on Thursday and Friday to go to the high school to help the marching band polish their formations for the Saturday game."

"But he sent me a note."

She shook her head. "Sorry, Jase. He's not here."

I raced through the school from the music rooms to the gym. No one was in the halls and they echoed strangely.

No one was in the locker room either. I dropped my books on the bench by my locker and reached for my lock. Thank goodness I always ran the combination through to the last number every time I put it on. All I had to do was pull.

My hand found only air. The lock was gone.

I checked the number—207. That was mine all right. Puzzled, I opened the door; nothing was inside. I looked at the number again. 207. What was going on?

I glanced up and down the alcove of lockers. There was no sign of my lock anywhere. As I began looking all over the locker room, in my mind I heard a time clock ticking loudly and saw Mr. Zindorf looking very unhappy, yelling, "Where's McCarver?" I finally found my lock hanging backward on a lock at the far end of the room. I didn't need many brains to figure out what was going on: Rand.

I sat on the bench in front of locker 623 and leaned backward so I could see the numbers when I pulled the lock away from the locker. After several failures, I finally opened the thing. I pulled the locker door open . . . *nothing!*

I was feeling slightly panicky. Where were my shoes and shorts and T-shirt and sweats? I raced around the room looking in all the cubbyholes and empty lockers. Zip.

Panic was a balloon blowing up in my stomach. I knew the team had to be finished with warm-ups and well into full practice by now. Mr. Zindorf was probably furious. I'd heard him let one kid have it for being late one day, and I didn't want the same thing to happen to me. I sure hoped Mike had told him about the note.

I stopped short. Of course. The note from Mr.

Keefer was a phony. Judy had never said he gave it to her. She'd just said it was for me. Rand had written it to drive me crazy at the least and to get me in trouble with Mr. Zindorf at the most. He'd definitely succeeded in his first goal, and I was afraid he would meet his second one, too, if I didn't get out there soon.

A great sadness settled over me, and I felt tears prick my eyes. When was this stuff going to end? I knew Mike would remind me that God was with me, even when I couldn't find my clothes.

"Well, God, since You're with me—and You did help me solve the genetics report problem—help me know what to do here, too. Please."

I knew I could never beat Rand at his own game. I wasn't nasty or devious like he was, and I didn't want to be. I wanted people to like me; I didn't want to pick on them and make them mad or hurt, not even Rand. Well, maybe Rand sometimes.

What should I do? I couldn't go out to Mr. Zindorf and cry my eyes out. It'd make me look like a fool and make Rand real happy. I couldn't just skip practice and make believe Rand hadn't done anything. That would make Rand happy, too, and besides, I wanted to play tomorrow.

As I sighed, I caught sight of a soccer shoe sitting on top of a row of lockers across the room.

"Bingo," I said aloud.

I climbed onto the bench by the appropriate locker and retrieved the shoe. Sure enough, it was mine. While I was up there, I looked around. I could see my other shoe, my shorts, sweats, and T-shirt all spread about the room on top of different lockers. Rand had been working hard.

I collected everything, changed, put my street clothes in my locker, and shut my lock. I did not spin any of the combination.

On the way out the door, an idea came. I smiled to myself. I would get Rand—who loved attention and credit—where it would bother him most.

When I reached the soccer field, Mr. Zindorf was standing not too far from the goal cage and Rand. I smiled to myself. Good.

"Mr. Zindorf," I said. "I apologize for being late. Mr. Keefer asked me to stop by his room after school, and I just got held up longer than I expected."

Out of the corner of my eye I could see Rand smirking. I ignored him and smiled at the coach. "I hope I haven't made a problem for you or for me by being this late."

Mr. Zindorf looked surprised. "No problem. Mike told me you'd received a note from Mr. Keefer. I appreciate your letting me know. I'll just speak to him about not asking you to stop by the day before a game."

"Yes," I said. "If you'd speak to him, that would be good." I nodded my head at the wisdom of his idea and saw Rand blanch a little. "Why don't I give you the note?" Rand began to look worried.

"Then you won't forget to talk to him."

"I think I can remember all by myself, Jase," Mr. Zindorf said. "Now you get in there at center forward."

"Yes, sir," I said. I ran out on the field as if I had had no greater problem today than tying my shoelaces. I said not one word to anyone about my locker or my clothes. I concentrated on playing and was delighted when I scored a goal off Rand.

"Hey, Rand," I yelled as he threw the ball back onto the playing field. "Great try!" And I grinned at him. He looked like a thundercloud.

I knew how to defang the snake. Don't react. Don't let him know he bothers you. Smile. Smile. Smile.

14

Finally, it was Friday and the Big Game. All of us on the team wore our team shirts to school, even Mike. They were navy blue with white stripes across the arms and had a white collar. Rand, as goalie, had a different shirt, navy and yellow striped like a huge bumble bee. We strutted around, revelling in everyone's we-know-you-can-beat-'em attitude. I just hoped we didn't have to crawl in Monday because we lost. I also hoped the rest of the season wouldn't be a letdown after all today's excitement.

Mom, Dad, and Matty were coming to the game as usual, and so were Mike's parents. He was sputtering with joy because they were coming.

"They never come to my things, Jase," he said on

the bus. "They're too career oriented. They say they're coming this time, but I'll believe it when I see it. At least they didn't say automatic no's as usual."

If Mike was pleased about his parents—who I hoped didn't have a fight in public—Rand was beside himself. He had walked over to our locker alcove to tell me and Mike and Fonz and Jeremy.

"My mom's coming," he said as we were getting dressed.

"Great, Rand," I said.

He was grinning and trying not to. He kept trying to zip his warm-up jacket—it took him four tries. Somehow I didn't think it was the game that was making him nervous.

Mom and Matty waved as we trotted onto the field. I noticed Matty was sitting by Mary Ellen again, and when the cheerleaders led the Every-Man cheer, Matty and Mary Ellen yelled, "Jason, Jason, he's our man. If he can't do it, no one can," louder than anyone. But I noticed Mary Ellen yelling her lungs out for Fonz, Jeremy, and—gag—Rand, too.

I looked around for a lady who looked like Rand, big and ugly, but I didn't see anyone. Probably she'd get there late, like Dad, because she had to work. I noticed Rand kept checking the bleachers all during warm-ups and the eighth grade game. When we took the field, his mom still wasn't there.

Mike's mom and dad were, though. When he

chased and retrieved his first out-of-bounds ball, they gave him a big cheer. He looked embarrassed, but I think he loved it.

It was a great game. I love to play when a team is clicking, and we were just right that afternoon. There were no glaring mental errors, no people out of position, no kicking shins and air instead of the ball. We controlled the ball most of the time, and while we had to fight for our scores, we were clearly the better team.

I personally got a great kick out of scoring two goals and hearing the crowd cheer.

I'll give Rand credit, he played a wonderful game. Our fullbacks are our weakest players, and it was Rand who saved our skin. His arms and legs seemed to grow as long as needed to make a save, then shrink back to normal size.

I noticed he kept glancing at the stands, and I did, too. I saw Dad arrive. I saw Mike's parents actually smile at each other as they got involved in the game. I saw Mary Ellen ruffle Matty's curls once, lucky kid. She was wearing the tricorn hat that he had worn as part of his Heritage Day costume. She looked cuter in it than he had when he'd marched off to school in the morning. Proud, too.

But I didn't see anyone who looked like Rand.

There were only two minutes remaining in the game when I kicked the ball to the right wing who missed it. It went sailing out of bounds and landed at the feet of a very pretty lady in a bright red dress who had just arrived. She squealed and dodged it, and the man in the business suit with her scooped it up and tossed it to Mike.

After the game Rand went running up to the red-dressed woman. He bent down and she pecked him on the cheek.

I'd never have picked her for his mom. First off, she was too tiny; second, she was too cute; third, she had too sweet a smile.

"You were wonderful, Randolph," she told him as we walked by. "Just wonderful! It was a great game."

I blinked. "A great game"? How did she know? She'd seen less than two minutes of it.

"We won, 4-1," Rand said proudly.

Rand, his mom and the man in the business suit fell into step behind Mom and me as we walked to the car, so I could hear their whole conversation. Matty and Dad were talking with Mike and his parents.

"It'll just take me a minute to get my stuff," Rand said to his mother, real happiness in his voice.

"Now, Randolph, don't hurry unless your ride is hurrying. I'm not going home." Ms. Purcell sounded so sweet and kind and reasonable.

"Oh." Rand sounded disbelieving and disappointed.

"Your ride hasn't left already, has it?" she asked.

"What if it has?" said Rand. "Would you take me home then?"

"I will ignore your nasty tone of voice, Randolph." She no longer sounded so sweet.

"I'm sure you will," said Rand. He was angry now. "You've had enough practice ignoring me."

"Randolph! Enough! You are certainly capable of putting a TV dinner in the oven by yourself." I doubt if a whip could have cut the air with more snap. "Bryan and I are going out for dinner." Suddenly her voice got sweet again. I figured she was now looking at Business-Suit-Bryan. "We just stopped to cheer you on."

"Wow, Mom, for a whole two minutes. I really am overwhelmed with gratitude, you know."

"Look, Randolph, I'll have you remember that I didn't have to stop at all. I only did it out of the goodness of my heart and because you begged."

Ms. Purcell's cutting tone didn't go with the smiling lady who squealed so daintily at the out-of-bounds ball. It went with an angry, selfish person who left her kid alone all the time.

I glanced at Mom who was walking beside me. Her face showed shock and sorrow. If Mom and Dad had felt bad for Rand before, I'd be lucky if they didn't ask him to move in now.

"Randolph, you give me nothing but trouble! Nothing I do pleases you!" She was hissing just like a goose.

"Then let me live with Grandmom and Pop!" Rand shouted.

There was silence for a moment behind us. Then

Rand spoke in a dead voice. "When will you be home?"

Ms. Purcell hesitated, probably to look at Business-Suit-Bryan for guidance. When she answered, the smile was back. "I have no idea. Now you just find your ride, and I'll see you tomorrow."

There was the sound of a kiss and a car door opening. Mom and I kept on until we reached her car. Dad and Matty joined us a minute later. I looked around, but I didn't see Rand.

"We've got to take Rand, Dad," I said. "His mom's not going home."

"That poor boy, Hal," said Mom.

"I know what you mean, dear," said Dad. "Why don't you and Matty go on home and get dinner going? Jase and I will see to Rand."

I went to the locker room and got my things without seeing Rand. I joined Dad at the car, and we waited for ten minutes. No one appeared to be left but the two of us, but we hadn't seen Rand leave with anyone.

"Jase," said Dad, "you'd better go check out the locker room again. I'd hate to leave if he was still here."

I jogged to the locker room and looked in. It was quiet and dark. I had just turned to leave when I heard a loud sniff. I stopped, startled, and listened intently. More sniffs. Someone was crying.

Suddenly the lockers erupted in a great rattling. Someone was beating on them.

Then there was silence again.

I peered carefully into the alcove where the noise was coming from. There stood Rand, head down, shoulders slumped, leaning against the lockers.

Ever so quietly I tiptoed back to the main door, wondering what to do. I certainly didn't want Rand to know I'd seen him crying. He'd be so upset that I knew he'd spend the rest of his life trying to get me.

Boy, I thought. There are a lot worse ways to reject someone than by placing him for adoption. There's every day rejection, and that's got to be the worst.

I grabbed the door and banged it loudly against the wall.

"Hey, Rand!" I yelled. "You in there?"

After a small silence, a surly voice answered, "You still here, shrimp?"

"Yeah. We're waiting for you."

"Be right there."

I turned and ran out to the car. By the time Rand climbed in the front, I was already safely seated in back. He stared out his window all the way to his empty house.

15

Soccer season finally wound to a close, Thanksgiving came and went, and I was chosen to play a solo in the Christmas music program.

I began trumpet lessons, and Mom found an old upright piano for seventy-five dollars. Dad's only complaint was that it cost one hundred dollars to move it to our house.

Mary Ellen was the light of my life, but I still got tongue-tied every time I tried to speak to her. Both she and Mike kept coming to the youth group. Mike definitely needed God's help when his father moved out, even if it was only for a weekend.

"Mike," I said on the bus ride home one December afternoon. "It's winter sports time."

Mike put down his computer magazine and looked at me. "And you, Mr. Short Person, are going to go out for basketball, right?"

"Never," I said. "What kind of a dummy do you think I am? Basketball's for big guys like Rand. Let's go out for wrestling."

"Do you mean you and me?" he asked in disbelief. "Us?"

I nodded. "I'll wrestle and you'll manage."

Mike made a face which clearly showed his feelings about being a wrestling manager.

"Come on, Mike. There won't be any balls to chase this time."

I saw a small—very small—lessening in his look of revulsion. I kept on pushing.

"When's the season begin?" he finally asked.

"Tomorrow," I said. "Come on. It'll be fun."

Mike snorted. Sweating was never fun as far as he was concerned, but I knew he'd give in sooner or later.

Sure enough, he did, and we showed up the next day to sign up with Mr. Freneau, the wrestling coach. What a pleasure to participate in a sport without my favorite enemy around to make life miserable. It was the beginning of a new and happy era.

"Hey, shrimp!"

My heart beat with distress. I turned. There stood Rand in all his arrogant glory.

"Why aren't you playing basketball?" I said.

"Are you strong enough to wrestle?" he asked. "A little guy like you?"

I sighed and looked at the ceiling.

Dear God, I thought, *not again. I suppose we'll have to give him a ride again after practices, too? Well, You got me through soccer without me losing my mind. I'm sure You'll get me through wrestling.*

I looked at Rand. "If you're smart enough to wrestle, I guess I'm strong enough. Come on, let's go practice."